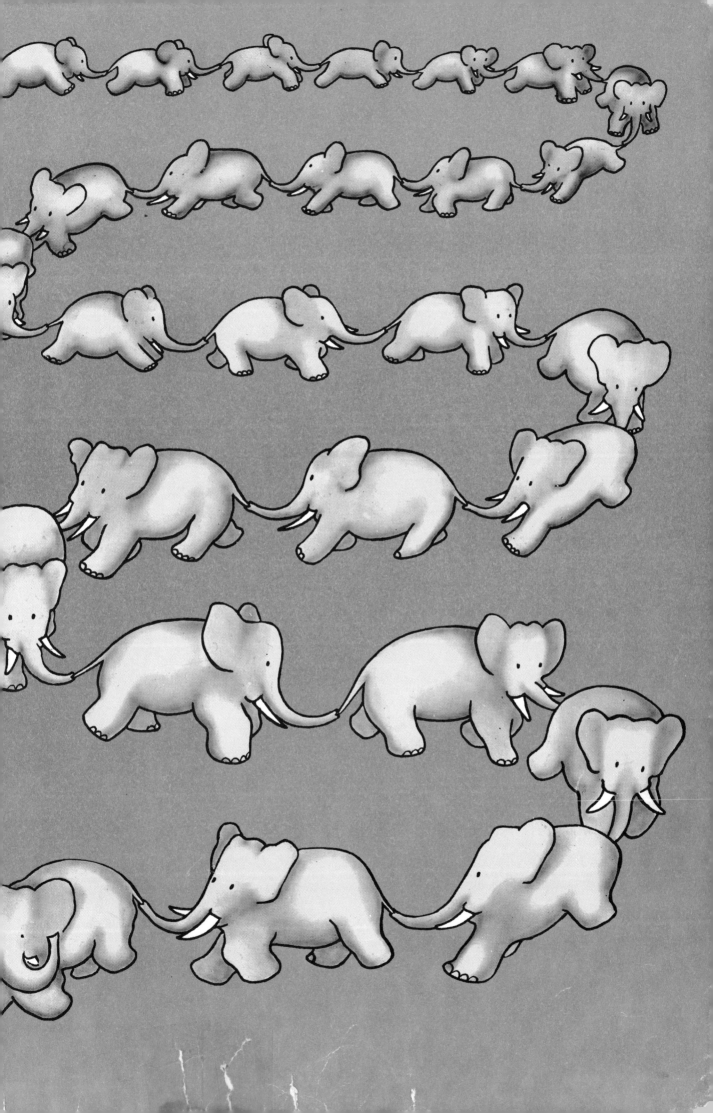

The Babar Books

The Story of Babar
The Travels of Babar
Babar the King
Babar and Zéphir
Babar and His Children
Babar and Father Christmas
Babar's Cousin: That Rascal Arthur
Babar's Fair
Babar and the Professor
Babar's Castle
Babar's French Lessons
Babar Comes to America
Babar's Spanish Lessons
Babar Loses His Crown
Babar's Trunk
Babar's Birthday Surprise
Babar Visits Another Planet
Meet Babar and His Family
Babar's Bookmobile
Babar and the Wully-Wully
Babar Saves the Day
Babar's Mystery
Babar Learns to Cook
Babar the Magician
Babar's Little Library
Babar and the Ghost
Babar's Anniversary Album

LAURENT DE BRUNHOFF

BABAR
COMES
TO AMERICA

Translated from the French
by M. JEAN CRAIG

RANDOM HOUSE

is title was originally cataloged by the Library of Congress as follows: Brunhoff, Laurent de, 1925— Babar comes to America. Translated from the French by M. Jean Cra
ew York] Random House [1965] 1 v. (unpaged) col. illus. 32 cm. I. Title.   PZ10.3.B7674 Baak   65—18163   ISBN 0-394-80588-7   0-394-90588-1 (lib. bd)

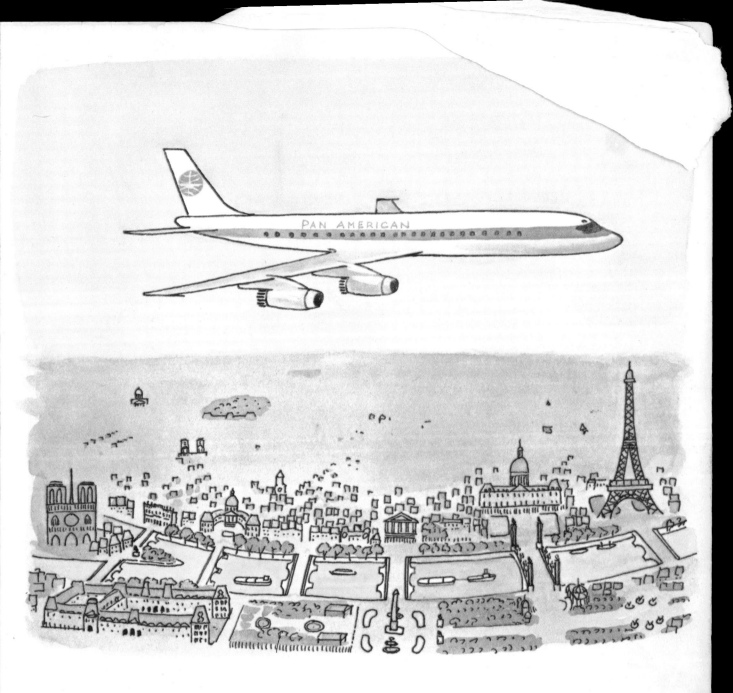

In an airplane flying over Paris, Babar, King of the Elephants, is on his way to the United States. The President has invited him for an official visit.

When little Alexander said, "I would like to go to America too!" Babar thought, "After all, why not?" And so it has been decided that Queen Celeste and the children will come later and will join Babar in California.

In just a few hours, the airplane is on the other side of the ocean. The stewardess announces through the loud-speaker: "Ladies and gentlemen, we are approaching Dulles International Airport, Washington, D.C. Fasten your seat belts, and please observe the no-smoking sign."

It is a very up-to-date airport. Traveling waiting rooms called mobile lounges, as comfortable as living rooms, carry passengers from the planes to the terminal building.

Surrounded by reporters and photographers, Babar says a few words in English, but with a strong French accent. "I am very happy to come to your great country, the country of Washington, of Mark Twain, of Danny Kaye . . ."

That same evening he has dinner with the President at the White House.

Babar goes to see the
Lincoln Memorial,

then the Jefferson Memorial,

and then the Capitol.
It is all very tiring.

Babar also visits the Washington Monument. After a few days he has visited all the museums in the capital. Here he is, gazing at a rocket outside the Smithsonian Institution.

"Do you have rockets like this in the country of the elephants?" someone asks.

"Of course," answers Babar. "The first astronaut to set foot on the moon might well be an elephant!"

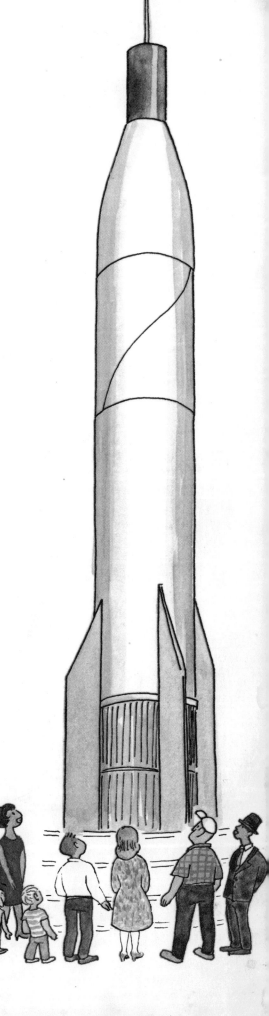

The official part of the trip is over. Babar is about to leave Washington to make a tour of the United States. So he packs away his crown and puts on a hat.

Then he flies to New York, a city he has always wanted to see. Babar feels happy and very excited.

As soon as he arrives, he goes for a walk on Park Avenue, but he gets something in his eye. This happens rather often in New York.

Babar has spent a restful night in the Hilton Hotel. Seated in front of the window, he has his breakfast of orange juice, toast, cereal, and tea.

Then he dresses quickly to go out. In the elevator he swallows several times to keep his ears from hurting. The fortieth floor is really very high!

Babar takes a bus. The driver scolds him for putting a quarter into the fare box instead of fifteen cents.

At the bus stop, the doors stay shut. Babar is worried.

"Step down!" shouts the driver. Babar steps down and the doors open automatically.

"A few seconds more, and I would have been trapped!" Babar thinks. Then he goes for a stroll in Central Park.

On the streets of New York, everyone seems
to be in a hurry. No one looks at anyone else.

And the moment the traffic lights turn green,
the auto horns all honk at once. What a racket!

Walking always makes Babar hungry. He goes into a drugstore.

He can't decide which to order—a hamburger or a cheeseburger. Finally he takes both. It is just as difficult to choose something to drink. He wants to try everything: Coca-Cola, Pepsi-Cola, V-8, 7 Up, ginger ale—all of them.

Finally, for dessert, he orders apple pie à la mode. But he samples a banana split and a chocolate soda, too. And then . . . he doesn't feel very well. He has eaten too much.

To buy something for his stomach ache, he just walks over to another counter in the same store. Drugstores are certainly convenient. It's too bad that there aren't any in the country of the elephants.

Now Babar continues his walk. He is looking for a jewelry store that has been recommended to him. But the store is gone. A new fifty-story building is being built here.

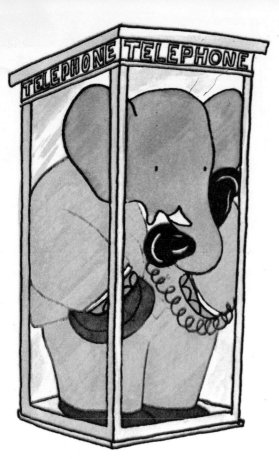

Suddenly Babar says to himself, "I have forgotten where I am supposed to meet my friends Bob and Helen!" He telephones them.

"We will pick you up at your hotel at seven o'clock," Helen says.

They take him to a Japanese restaurant. Babar is delighted with it. He takes off his shoes like everyone else.

Babar tells his friends that he has bought a brass rooster in an antique shop.

Later in the evening, they go to Greenwich Village to hear Theodorus Priest and his quartet.

Bob asks, "Do you like jazz?" "Very much," says Babar.

Babar spends a quiet weekend in Scarsdale with his friends and their children, Peter, Tommy, Billy, and the dog, Sadie.

Babar learns to play baseball. What strength! And he doesn't even need a glove to catch the ball.

"It's not fair," says little Billy.

"Would you like to go to the supermarket with me?" asks Helen. "With pleasure," answers Babar. "And I will push the shopping cart." But he has a hard time following Helen as she quickly makes her way through the aisles.

Babar takes home some popcorn for Peter, Tommy, and Billy.

"This way, I'm over here," she calls to him. Forgetting that he is so big, Babar knocks over a gallon of cider.

The bottle breaks. There is quite a traffic jam. Babar is very upset. "It's not important," Helen says to console him.

In the evening they watch a baseball game on television.

Babar has spent a whole evening preparing for the rest of his trip, and deciding which places to visit.

He goes to Boston, and then to Harvard University nearby.

Babar is awarded the degree of Doctor of Letters, a great honor. The professors present him with his diploma and his hood.

Then Babar visits the office of the "Lampoon," the student magazine. He promises to send the students photographs from the country of the elephants.

Babar continues on his tour. Here he is in Detroit, inspecting an automobile factory. It is certainly fascinating to learn how cars are made.

First there is only a block of red-hot steel.

It is cut up and shaped into many parts, and then every-thing is put together on the assembly line.

Suddenly Babar hears someone shout, "Watch out, Mr. Elephant!"

Too late! His hat is gone . . .

Babar admires Chicago, especially the Merchandise Mart

and the Marina Towers. Here he is on State Street.

On Sunday some friends take Babar fishing on the shore of
Lake Michigan. There are a great many people. They all
have fishing rods, picnic
lunches, barbecue grills, and
even television sets. Babar
settles down to fish. For a
long time he must be pa-
tient.

It really seems that there
are no fish . . .
Still nothing . . .

Oops! There is one on his hook! But to serve for lunch it is rather small. "You won't starve, Babar," his friend Lena says. "I have brought a steak."

In fact, no one beside the lake is eating fish! Everywhere are barbecue grills with skewered meat and spare ribs.

Babar broils the steak like a real chef. After lunch he plays with Lena's little boy Adrian.

Babar continues his trip west. The train takes him across
the Rocky Mountains.

Babar rides in the Vistadome car so that he can admire the view and take photographs.

Babar arrives at the hotel in San Francisco.

"There he is!" shout Pom, Flora, Alexander, and Cousin Arthur, who have been hiding on the staircase.

"Papa!"

"Babar!"

The manager welcomes Babar, and the children take him to his room, where Celeste is waiting. Babar kisses her tenderly. Then Flora and Alexander jump into his lap, insisting, "Tell us about your trip!"

Babar tells them about everything he has done since his arrival in Washington. Then he goes out to see the Golden Gate Bridge. Unfortunately, it is hidden by fog. Babar must go back three times before the weather is clear.

"This bridge is as beautiful as a cathedral," he thinks to himself.

This is how a family of elephants rides on a cable car, to keep it from tipping over. Celeste and Flora have taken a taxi, because women are not permitted to ride on the outside of the cable car.

On Telegraph Hill, Alexander has a naughty idea. "Why don't we put on our roller skates?" he suggests.

Babar and Celeste are just wondering where Arthur, Pom, and Alexander have gone, when they suddenly appear, rolling down the street at full speed. A policeman catches them, and warns them not to do it again.

Babar is sketching on Fisherman's Wharf. Pom, who has come with him, suddenly begins to cry.

"My stomach hurts!" he moans.

Babar carries Pom back to the hotel on his shoulder. The little elephant is still crying.

Celeste calls the doctor.
"My child," says the doctor, taking Pom's pulse, "you have eaten too much lobster. That's all there is to it."

Pom has to take bad-tasting medicine, and he grumbles a little. But he wants to get well, so he does what he is told.

When Pom is bet-
ter, they go for a
ride along the coast
of the Pacific, and
stop to watch the
seals and the birds
through binoculars.
The seals bark in
a very odd way.

"I'd love to take one home," says Pom.

"It wouldn't be happy," says Arthur. "A seal must live
in the water."

"Too bad," says Pom. "Then how about a pelican?"

Stopping at the delightful little town of Carmel, Babar and his family settle down in a cottage by the sea.

Babar and Arthur have a good time riding the surf.

The children like to jump into the big waves, and to gather seaweed and shells. Flora prefers to go for walks in the garden of the Spanish church, which is full of flowers and tiny hummingbirds.

Babar and his family have left Carmel to visit Yosemite Park. What wonderful mountains!

When the car drives through a tremendous sequoia, Pom asks, "How did they make this hole?"

And Flora worries: "Suppose the tree should fall while we are passing beneath it!"

This is Death Valley. Since the sun is blazing hot, Celeste has brought along her umbrella.

Arthur wants to photograph the whole family beside Bad Water pool. He sets up his automatic camera and hurries to stand next to Flora, so that he can be in the picture too.

Oh, Los Angeles! It is so big that one cannot tell where it begins or where it ends. Babar doesn't believe his eyes. "Everyone told us that we would lose our way among all

these highways," he says to himself. "Well, I'm quite proud of myself. It seems to me that I manage very well indeed."

A famous moving-picture director, Urchin Walls, gives a reception at his house in Beverly Hills in honor of Babar and Celeste. Some of the movie stars are there.

Babar has promised to take the children to Disneyland. But it is a long way. To get there, one must pass forests of telegraph poles and armies of oil-well pumps. The pumps, rocking back and forth without stopping, look like enormous birds pecking away.

At last, Disneyland! Pom, Flora, and Alexander are trembling with excitement.

They run along Main Street toward Sleeping Beauty's Castle. They hurl themselves into the toboggans of the Matterhorn. Then they spin in the Mad Teacups until their heads are whirling. And, like all the passengers aboard the sternwheel steamboat, they feel they are actually on the Mississippi River.

There is so much to see that one day is not nearly
enough.

"It is time to go back now," says Celeste. "I'm too tired
for any more, and I'm sure you are too."

Alexander protests: "I wanted so badly to ride in the
submarine!"

In North Hollywood, Charles and Liza have a wonderfully blue swimming pool. Pom, Flora, Alexander, and Arthur spend most of their time in it, swimming like fish.

"When you decide to take your turn at diving, Babar," Liza says jokingly, "let me know. I'll have to lower the water level, or else the pool will overflow and the whole garden will be flooded!"

One evening they all go to see a movie at a drive-in. The children love it, especially since they have a picnic supper in the car.

Celeste and the children are going to stay a few days
longer in Los Angeles before returning to New York.

Babar and Arthur leave by helicopter—each in his own, because together they would be too heavy for one.

While they are flying over the Arizona desert, Babar runs out of gas. He comes down in the middle of some cactus.

Arthur lands close by. "What is the matter?" he shouts.

While Babar waits, seated on a rock, Arthur flies off to look for gas. But at the very moment that he sees a service station in the distance, he runs out of gas too.

"What luck!" he groans. "A whole mile to walk in this sun, carrying two cans of gas. I don't much care for this!"

They have arrived at the Grand Canyon. Arthur wants to
go down to the Colorado River. Since they do not wish to
crush the mules, they go on foot. Wisely, Babar suggests
that they call a halt before they reach the bottom:

"Remember, climbing up again is much harder."

At sunset they admire the view. "All the same," thinks
Arthur, "it's a bit too big."

Babar and Arthur pay a visit to the Indians.

They listen, fascinated, to the hunting tales told by old Chief Sitting Bull. He also tells them the legend of the White Buffalo.

Arthur dances while Babar thumps on a big drum.

"You dance almost as well as we do," the Indians say politely.

Babar and Arthur are now in Texas. In Dallas, Babar buys a checked shirt.

They go to see a ranch where there are magnificent Black Angus cattle.

"I'm going to show you the finest bull in the world," the cowboy says. "He is called Max. If I scratch his back, he shakes his head like a big dog."

New Orleans! This is their last stop before returning to New York. The two travelers ride in a carriage through the old French Quarter.

"Those little balconies are really charming," say Babar.

Finally, in an excellent restaurant, they feast on fried chicken and pecan pie.

In the fall, everyone stops playing baseball and starts playing football. Babar and Arthur, who have joined Celeste and the children in New York, go to New Haven. Bob and Helen take them to the Harvard-Yale game.

Peter, Tommy, and Billy are there too.

"Come on, Harvard! Hit them again! Harder!"

But at the half, Yale is ahead. The bands march across the field.

After the game Arthur learns how to play football.

He can play European rugby, but football rules are different.

Arthur manages quite well. He is heavy, and it is not easy to stop him.

The Yale and Harvard teams play with Arthur a few minutes, just for fun.

"But no matter how heavy I am," thinks the young elephant, "there's nothing much I can do when a whole team jumps on me!"

On Thanksgiving, Bob and Helen invite Babar and his family to join them for dinner.

They ask the King of the Elephants if he will carve the turkey.

Celeste is hurrying to buy some last-minute gifts. As she passes the hat department, she cannot resist the temptation to choose a new one for herself.

And now it is time to pack, and to say good-by.

Babar, Celeste, Arthur, Pom, Flora, and Alexander are returning to the country of the elephants. They are sad about leaving, but they hope to see their friends again someday.

On the deck of the ship, watching the tall buildings fade slowly into the distance, they carry with them the memories of their wonderful trip to America.